MW01141761

Seymour's Masquerade Ball

Written and
Illustrated
by
Sally O. Lee

Copyright@2006 Sally C
All Rights Reserv
ISBN 1-4196-280
Seymour's Masqu

I would like to thank Stephanie Robinson and the staff at
BookSurge for their encouragement in helping
me to write and illustrate this book.

www.booksurge.com

Also, I would like to thank my family and friends
for their love and support.

This book is typeset in Garamond and Lucy.

www.leepublishing.net

o: Mom and Dad

Copyright @ 2006, Sally O. Lee, All rights reserved.

ne day,
Lucy and Seymour
were playing with
their favorite yellow ball.

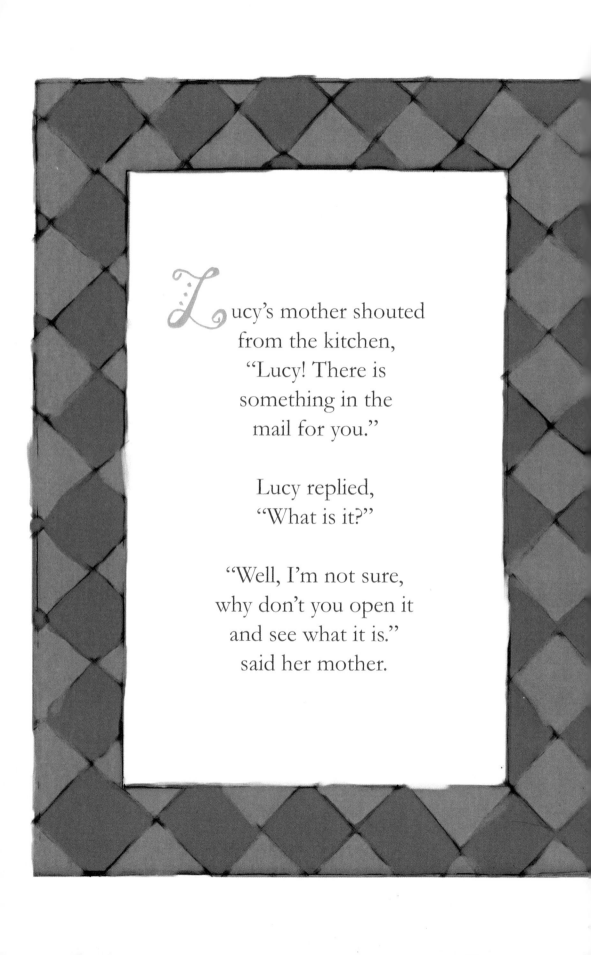

Lucy's mother shouted
from the kitchen,
"Lucy! There is
something in the
mail for you."

Lucy replied,
"What is it?"

"Well, I'm not sure,
why don't you open it
and see what it is."
said her mother.

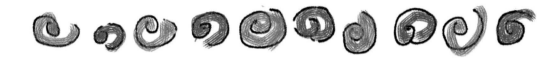

So, Lucy took the envelope
from her mother and
opened it.

Inside was the most
beautiful invitation that
Lucy and Seymour
had ever seen.

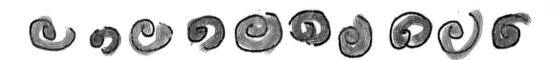

To: Lucy and Seymour you are Cordially invited to a Masquerade Ball

So Lucy and
Seymour searched in her closet
for something to wear to the ball.

But when they went to her closet
and opened the doors,
there were no ball gowns there.

There were no shiny shoes or
sparkly dresses or fancy hats.

There were no tuxedos or big bow ties.

"What are we going to do, Seymour?"
Lucy asked.
"We have no costumes
for the masquerade ball."

Seymour looked at Lucy
with wonder.

They decided to search in the attic.

They found an old chest filled
with clothes, shoes, and even some jewels.

Seymour found a black tuxedo.

And Lucy found a red dress.

Lucy and Seymour put on
their masquerade costumes.

And holding on very tightly to
their invitations,
they went to the ball.

One by one, the guests arrived
wearing fancy dresses, velvet jackets,
sparkly masks, twinkly shoes,
and silk sashes.

They arrived in grand shiny cars with
big fenders and black and
silver wheels that glittered
in the sun.

Perry, the proud pig,
arrived at the
ball in his fancy purple car.

Danforth, the dragon,
arrived in a
turquoise velvet jacket with a
fancy orange bow tie.

Pierre,
the penguin,
arrived not
having to wear
any costume at all!

Harriett the hare stood up and announced to the guests, "Welcome to the masquerade ball! I am so glad that all of you could attend....

We have many surprises in store for you. There are prizes and and games for everyone!...And, a prize will be given for the best masquerade costume."

All the guests cheered. They wondered who would win the prize. They paraded around the grand lawn in their masquerade costumes so that all could see.

Harriett the hare stood in front of everyone and said,

"We have a winner for the
Best Masquerade Costume!"

The guests gathered around, and it was very quiet.
Lucy and Seymour were sure that they would not
win since they had found their costumes in an old
box in the attic. They were sure that Danforth would
win with his fancy orange tie. Or that Pierre
would win with his elegant tuxedo. Or that Harriett
would win with her sparkly satin dress.

"The winners of the Best Masquerade
Costume Contest are Lucy and Seymour!
Congratulations!" Harriett exclaimed.

Lucy and Seymour jumped up and down.
They could not believe that they had won.
"Now, we will all eat cake and
celebrate the winners!"

Lucy and Seymour ran and found the cake.
It was the biggest cake they had ever seen.
It was three times as big as Seymour!

Everyone gathered around the cake and looked at it with awe. There were pink layers, and green layers, purple layers and yellow layers. It was covered in frosting of every color with sparkling candles on the top.

They all ate a piece of cake, and it was the most delicious cake they had ever eaten.

It was the best masquerade ball ever.

Brownsville Community Library
P.O. Box 68
Brownsville, OR 97327

02 2014